Illumen
Spring 2024

Edited by
Tyree Campbell

Illumen
Spring 2024

Edited by Tyree Campbell

Cover art "Shackleton's Last Folly" by Lorraine Pinelli Brown
Cover design by Laura Givens

Vol. XXI, No. 3   April 2024
Illumen [ISSN: 1558-9714] is published quarterly on the 1st days of January, April, July, and October in the United States of America by Hiraeth Publishing, P.O. Box 1248, Tularosa, NM 88352. Copyright 2024 by Hiraeth Publishing. All rights revert to authors and artists upon publication except as noted in selected individual contracts. Nothing may be reproduced in whole or in part without written permission from the authors and artists. Any similarity between places and persons mentioned in the fiction or semi-fiction and real places or persons living or dead is coincidental. Writers and artists guidelines are available online at www.hiraethsffh.com/blank-page. Guidelines are also available upon request from Hiraeth Publishing, P.O. Box 1248, Tularosa, NM 88352, if request is accompanied by a SASE #10 envelope with a 60-cent US stamp. Editor: Tyree Campbell. Subscriptions: $28 for one year [4 issues], $54 for two years [8 issues]. Single copies $10.00 postage paid in the United States. Subscriptions to Canada: $32 for one year, $54 for two years. Single copies $12.00 postage paid to Canada. U.S. and Canadian subscribers remit in U.S. funds. All other countries inquire about rates.

New from Terrie Leigh Relf!!
Postcards From Space

Terrie Leigh Relf loves sending and receiving postcards from the four corners of the universe—and beyond! Postcards tell a story. They are mementos from friends and family—and from total strangers—and provide a glimpse into life's journeys, observations, and adventures.

Here are some messages on postcards from space, found aboard a derelict craft that crashed on an arid, lifeless world. The OSPS (Outer Space Postal Service) has delivered these messages to Terrie, who now presents them to you. This is what it is like out there.

https://www.hiraethsffh.com/product-page/postcards-from-space-by-terrie-leigh-relf

A Little Help, Please

In the world of the small indie press we fight a never-ending battle for attention to our work, as writers and in publishing. Here's an example: big publishers [you know who they are] have gobs of $$$ that they can devote to advertising and marketing. Here at Hiraeth Publishing, our advertising budget consists of the deposits for whatever soda bottles and aluminum cans we can find alongside the highways. Anti-littering laws make our task even more difficult . . . ☺

That's where YOU come in. YOU are our best promoter. YOU are the one who can tell others about us. Just send 'em to our website, tell them about our store. That's all. Just that.

Of course, we don't mind if you talk us up. We're pretty good, you know. We have some award-winning and award-nominated writers and artists, plus other voices well-deserving to be heard [not everyone wins awards, right?] but our publications are read-worthy nevertheless.

That number once again is:

www.hiraethsffh.com

Friend us on Facebook at Hiraeth Publish and follow us on Twitter at

@HiraethPublish1

Contents

Features
16 The Guy Belleranti Page
41 Who's Who

Poems
12 Alien Lady in a Silk Robe by Darrell Lindsey
14 When the Villagers Come by Jacqueline West
17 Another Chapter of Life by Amirah al-Wassif
18 A Poem for Hypnos by Stephanie Smith
20 The Master's Mate by Lee Clark Zumpe
22 Dead Butterfly by Stephanie Smith
   The Apex Predator by Alan Ira Gordon
24 The Age of Innocence by Amirah al-Wassif
25 roses for the hanged man & lilies for his wife by Zoe Davis
28 Water Striders by Debby Feo
   Metamorphosis by Debby Feo
29 Winter Guest by Jacqueline West
30 Winter Roads by K. S. Hardy
   2 Ku by K. S. Hardy
31 Eddie's Bar, Pt. 2 by Matthew Roy
34 Wind Witch by K. S. Hardy
35 Mother of Monsters by Matthew Roy
38 Poison Princess by Allister Nelson
40 The Rules of Blind Obedience by Amirah al-Wassif

Illustrations
13 Goddess of Animals by Sandy DeLuca
18 Night of the Raven by Sandy DeLuca
33 Woman of the Dead by Sandy DeLuca

SUBSCRIBE TO ILLUMEN!!

We'll be glad you did...
So will you.
Here's the link:

https://www.hiraethsffh.com/product-page/illumen-1

Support the small independent press!

You're not afraid of a little poetry, are you?

The Miseducation of the Androids
By William Landis

What happens when androids confront concepts inconsistent with their programming? William Landis examines this question by means of flash fiction and haiku that you will find pithy, poignant, and amusing.

William Landis is a science fiction poet from North Carolina. He is a graduate of North Carolina A&T State University, completing both undergraduate, and graduate work in agriculture. He is currently working on a vermicomposting project, and he is an Army reserve engineer officer. He enjoys running, writing, reading, and exploring new places.

Order a copy here: https://www.hiraethsffh.com/product-page/miseducation-of-the-androids-by-william-landis

Midnight Comes Early
By Marcie Lynn Tentchoff

Marcie Lynn Tentchoff lives on the west coast of Canada, in a forest of brambles and evergreens far too densely tangled to form the setting for any but the darkest of fairy tales. She writes poetry and stories that tiptoe worriedly along the border of speculation and horror, and is an active member of both the Science Fiction & Fantasy Poetry Association and the Horror Writers Association. Marcie is an Aurora Award winner, and her work has been either nominated, short, or long-listed for Stoker, Rhysling, and British Fantasy awards. She is very much involved in middle grade and YA media, and edits Spaceports & Spidersilk, a magazine aimed at readers from 8-9 up to (and past!) 89. When she is not involved with the practice of placing and editing words on a page, she teaches creative writing and acting for a performing arts studio.

Order a copy here...

https://www.hiraethsffh.com/product-page/midnight-comes-early-by-marcie-lynn-tentchoff

In Days to Come
By Lisa Timpf

The poems in this collection are grouped into four sections. The first, "Terra, Terra," includes poems set on the planet Earth. That is true of many of the poems in the second section, "Looming Shadows," though they have been grouped together in relation to some of the potential disasters we as a human race have set ourselves up for—nuclear warfare, climate change, and so on. "Alien Encounters" contains poems relating to imagined interactions with other space-faring species. "Other Worlds" rounds out the collection with speculations on what life might be like if and when humanity spins out to the stars.

Order a copy here...
https://www.hiraethsffh.com/product-page/in-days-to-come-by-lisa-timpf

Alien Lady in a Silk Robe
Darrell Lindsey

She spun a sun with golden thread
and hung it in a ripe sky,
taught the wind to sing again
through trees she dreamed back to life.

Those called nobles tried to chain her thrice
for doing what they could not,
for all they had created
was bedlam, and nightmares, and rot.

She said she would build a palace
known throughout the universe,
one with enough silver and steel
to extinguish every future curse.

And though a vast army invaded,
it was but a spit of fire,
for the heavens had been unleashed
and other powers were only ankle high.

Goddess of Animals
Sandy DeLuca

When the Villagers Come
Jacqueline West

From a distance,
it's breathtaking.
A river of stars, a flood
of fireflies glimmering
over black hillsides.
Pilgrims, you might think,
chanting, holding candles.
You might let yourself believe.
You watch from the tower window
because you've never seen
anything so lovely, and because
there is nothing else to do;
you're tired of everything
but the spell of that light
winding toward your cracked
stone walls. Your spine
has stooped with the years,
your bone-snapping hands
curling inward like roots.
Even your eyes, once so sharp
in the dark, are dulling now,
letting you see an onrush
of flame as welcome, wondrous,
wonderful, when at last
you're washed in that bright
river, caught inside that swarm
of wings. When your own heart burns
in the heart of those stars.

Candle and Pins
Poems on Superstitions
By Jacqueline West

The poems of "Candle and Pins" are inspired by familiar—and some unfamiliar—superstitions, ranging from love charms to burial practices, parsley seeds to the evil eye. Like superstitions themselves, these poems explore the terrain where magic and everyday life intertwine, and where beauty, horror, fear, and belief combine in ways both new and ageless.

https://www.hiraethsffh.com/product-page/candles-and-pins-by-jacqueline-west

The Guy Belleranti Page

frosty full moon night
she shivers in lover's arms
as he grows wolf coat

Saturn iPhone
a universe favorite
beautiful ringtones

mad ventriloquist
eager to speak new voices
sends dummy to school

my alien friend
impervious to vampires
has ice in veins

Another Chapter of Life
Amirah al-Wassif

When the sky falls down,
Another chapter of life will soon open
The butterflies would love to jump
And the frogs would wish to fly
Me and you will soon melt
In one cup of thoughts and feelings
 I will be there waiting for you
In a porch covered by caramel
There, my right hand on my chest
Breathing through air made of poetry
 I am touched by generous spirits
And thankful delights.
When the sky falls down,
A great gate will soon appear
 In the midst of nowhere
And a holy voice from the upstairs
Will call us
"Come here, come here
This is the end of the life Circus"
Then we all will obey
Satisfaction will water our thirsty souls
We all here bathe under heavenly showers
I will not text anyone about the climate change
 I will not cry because of racism
I will not lie in my bed
Watching the breaking news.

I will not suffer anymore
Here, just me and you dwell in the honey rivers
The delicious touch our fingers sweetly
Here, where no sky
The curtains of eternal love
Wave to us like a very long kiss
The soul and these distant things
That longed for.

A Poem for Hypnos
Stephanie Smith

Somewhere between
Insomnia and heavy machinery
A crack of light appears
There is a space inside darkness
Where all the stars go reeling
I see shapes in the sound of the spheres
I cannot know if I am awake or dreaming
If I have fallen into that place
Where lullabies grow teeth
And tear my bedsheets to shreds
I puncture a hole in the universe
With my thoughts

Night of the Raven
Sandy DeLuca

the master's mate
Lee Clark Zumpe

The master's mate, they say, worked the pumps,
down below, in those shadow-haunted lower decks,
lingering long after he had cleared the corridors
of terrified cadets too young to perish.

The master's mate, they say, propped up the hull,
applying cutting-edge technology and practical physics
to buy the passengers precious moments
to make their way to the lifepods.

The master's mate, they say, joined the captain,
pale and worn, on the bridge of the *Fairstar*,
relieved the evacuation had been a success,
saddened by the repercussions of the accident.

The master's mate, they say, in his final moments,
as the colony transport disintegrated,
affirmed his love for his wife and children,
and wished them long, happy lives on Mars.

Wearing Winter Gray
By Lee Clark Zumpe

Atmospheric poetry at its finest is found in Wearing Winter Gray. Lee Clark Zumpe sets his moods and draws forth evocative images and memories, and not a little emotion. Now and then a ray of light shines through his words, so that having created a somber mood, he punctuates it with a bit of joy. Thus it is that Wearing Winter Gray reminds us that Shiny Summer Colors are just around the corner.

Print: https://www.hiraethsffh.com/product-page/wearing-winter-gray-by-lee-clark-zumpe
ePub: https://www.hiraethsffh.com/product-page/wearing-winter-gray-by-lee-clark-zumpe-2
PDF: https://www.hiraethsffh.com/product-page/wearing-winter-gray-by-lee-clark-zumpe-1

Dead Butterfly
Stephanie Smith

I fail in matters of cause and effect
These tattered wings lead me nowhere
Holes are torn in my universe
Encouraging new worlds to be born

I am the storm and the calm before it
The thunder and the rain
Pain explodes from my fingertips
Raging hot as the blood in my veins

I am all the colors of the rainbow
My palette never runs dry
I paint life like a butterfly:
Here one day but gone the next

The Apex Predator
Alan Ira Gordon

Vacuuming through the endless starlanes
and sundry solar systems, ignoring
nonsentient species and primitive
races; focused on eliminating
only those advanced enough to achieve
parity and rivalry.

And thus a true threat.

Planet Hunter
By Alan Ira Gordon

Get a copy here...

https://www.hiraethsffh.com/product-page/planet-hunters-by-alan-ira-gordon

The Age of Innocence
Amirah al-Wassif

When the planet earth swallows all the maps,
The love affection will spread everywhere
I will hang out in your precious land
And you will spend your night
Pacing my room back and forth.
When the maps disappear,
We will replace our fingers with flowers
You will not call me Negro
And I will not laugh at your grandfather's roots.
When the planet earth
Swallows all the maps
We will write our history
By an honest ink
If this happened
People in Madagascar
Will not eat dirt
To escape hunger
When the maps disappear,
I will give you my tongue
To speak my language
And the humanity
Will be the native one
For all of us.

roses for the hanged man & lilies for his wife
Zoe Davis

the villagers
were surprised
when flowers
grew from the
hanged man

his crow-pecked sockets
slackened maw dripping
roots like soft regrets

a single daisy
sprung
from
sun-bleached hand
an offering

for his sweetheart
for his absolution
his cage

no longer
a gibbet but a
hanging
basket

Minimalism:
A Handbook of Minimalist Genre Poetic Forms

This handbook contains articles about how to write various minimalist poetry forms such as scifaiku, senryu, sijo, haibun, empat perkataan, ghazals, cinquain, cherita, rengays, rengu, octains, tanka, threesomes, and many more. Each article is written by an expert in that particular poetry form.

Teri Santitoro, aka sakyu, who assembled this handbook, has been the editor of Scifaikuest since 2003.

https://www.hiraethsffh.com/product-page/minimalism-a-handbook-of-minimalist-genre-poetic-forms

Water Striders
Debby Feo

A popular swimming hole
Under ancient lunar dome
Water scooped up from Earth but
Contaminated in Space

Irradiated insects
Attracted to any splash
Swarmed and consumed unwary
Leaving sunken skeletons

Metamorphosis
Debby Feo

I'm crawling out of my skin
Not metaphorically
Claustrophobia winning
Ripping open from within

Following unpleasant dreams
Of eating until engorged
Sputum covering myself
Hanging from sturdy limb

Completed my mutation
Emerging from my cocoon
And in the orangish haze
Flapping to dry my wings

Winter Guest
Jacqueline West

We thought it was just the cold
that had turned her that unsettling color—

lips grayish and sealed with frost, skin
the hue of a robin's egg under snow.

We brought her inside, steered her
to the fire, rubbed at her bare hands and feet

none of us saying aloud until too late
that she kept surprisingly still.

We were familiar with frostbite and fevers,
with the heaviness that can sing you to sleep

in a snowbank even while eating your limbs away.
We knew about water, about patience and time.

By night, we were sure we knew her too—
this tall, quiet thing hunched in our best chair,

the hands that clasped its carved arms tight,
white fingernails leaving tracks in the wood.

We were sure that we had saved her,
convinced ourselves that her skin looked rosier now

that it wasn't still the milk-blue of porcelain,
that the breath passing between her sharp teeth

was not as cold as January air. That her eyes,
when they moved, weren't following us.

Moon Roads
K. S. Hardy

A spiderweb of light
Enshrouds the landscape,
Radiating out to the
Distant horizon,
Leading where no
Wise one knows
But taking those
With the brave heart
And the silver luck
Where their hopes
And dreams may lead.

2 Ku
K. S. Hardy

Embroidered with stars
Woven by string theory
Dark cloth of the void

Dawn mists in graveyards
Ghosts returning to bed
No eternal rest

Eddie's Bar Pt. 2
Matthew Roy

What Is Eddie's?
It is a bar at the end of the world. Take that how you will.
A last blue-collar pitstop at the edge of all that is known or simply a time and place mired in the death-throe countdown of all that came before.

Terminus est either way.

It is phantasmagoria. It glints like golden teeth and slowly fades like deathshroud gauze.
Broken-down, dying timeclock men, revenants with grimy denim collars, gather for a drink before summoning the courage to go home.

So filthy from muck and factory oil as to be indistinguishable from one another, doomed refuse in the shape of men.
With the right kind of eyes, though, you could see their souls shining through like arc lights.
But the right kind of eyes are hard to come by in this knockemstiff world.

At the center of it all, eddie the bartender, a working-class hades, both a person and a place, presiding over a beer-stained underworld.

Old souls and old pros.
Old prose.
Worthless words.

These men know some basic truths:

1. The sink and sway of eddie's warped floorboards as they stumble out back to piss.
2. The lung disease laugh of the lifetime smoker at the end of the bar.
3. The way a little bit of liquid poison leaves you invigorated, if only for a while.

A daemon with hunched shoulders sits at the end of the bar, stirring a straw in a whiskey and coke, looking down and losing himself in the slow black spiral of his third drink of the night. Later tonight, he'll send a drunken text to an ex-girlfriend.

See the hangdog angels at the back table finish their drinks, one more for the road, and lift themselves with shaky dignity and more grace than these drunks could ever muster, rising on shabby wings,
Passing translucent through the ceiling and into the sky, their sandals peeling off a sticky floor as they rise.
High as astronauts drinking beer from aluminum cans, floating in the taste of metal and recycled air. Humid from human breath.

This place should be condemned – like its patrons – but who's left to do the condemning?
These are the only men left in the world.
Drinking at Eddie's Bar.

Woman of the Dead
Sandy DeLuca

Wind Witch
K. S. Hardy

Her dress is woven
From cumulus clouds
Her hair is dark
As a driven storm
Her skin as pale
White as moon snow

She calls the winds
From every corner
Of the confused compass
They are her servants
Slaves of her desire
To do her bidding
To carry her softly
All around the globe
Or to wreak hurricane
Havoc on those fools
Who displease her.

Mother Of Monsters
Matthew Roy

Did you know that all the beasts
That heracles killed in his labors –
The nemean lion,
Whose pelt he skinned and wore;
The baleful hydra and ladon the dragon;
Cerberus, the hound of the underworld,
Among others – were siblings,
Had the same mother and father?
Their parents were echidna,
The beautiful serpent-woman,
And typhon, the tireless giant.

Among the complicated love lives
Of the ancient greek pantheon,
Where lustful zeus would sleep
With any woman he could catch
(by charm or force or guile),
With the gods and their affairs
And complicated family trees
(half-siblings and whatnot),
Echidna and typhon stayed true to each other,
A lone example of fidelity in an
Outrageously polyamorous world,
A stable home for a dreadful,
Growing brood.

And a then madman named heracles,
Believing each murder would
Help absolve him of some sin,

Slew their children, one after the other
After the other.
Echidna and typhon's little ones
Were nothing but tests, challenges,
Labors to heracles.

Imagine the grief in the aftermath of that!
Echidna receiving all those telegrams
On the same day
Like the mother of the sullivan boys.
Every mother grieves the loss of her children,
Even a mother of monsters.
And it wasn't like her children
Were terrorizing the countryside
Or kidnapping fair maidens
Or something like that.
Most were simple security guards,
Watching over apples or sacred trees
Or the land of the dead.

My father, trying to support his family,
Once took a side job as a night watchman,
And i can't imagine the shock-horror i'd have felt
If he'd been killed some night
By a muscle-bound lunatic in lionskin underwear,
Who was trying to tick an item off a list
To get absolution for slaughtering
His own wife and kids.

But i guess that's it, right?
The children of monsters,
The offspring of the poor and disenfranchised,
Are only made to be villains
And background characters,
Bystanders in someone else's drama,

Like mass shooting victims
Or the townsfolk swept away by a landslide.
Meanwhile, we follow the fashionable
And dramatic lives of the nepo-babies
Of gods and movie stars on social media
And in tell-alls
And in the myths
We pass down through the ages.

But i'm telling you to remember
The grieving mothers and fathers,
The serpent-women and tireless giants,
Who did their best, picked up second jobs
And kept late nights,
Up with crying infant monsters,
Who dreamed of better lives
And brighter futures
When they looked upon their playing children,
Who doted on and poured their affection
Into their beloved, ghastly sons and daughters.

Poison Princess
Allister Nelson

Did you get everything you wanted, Briar Rose? Two suckling babes at your breast, a blind prince who found his sight again in your roses, seeds of the dog thorns and wolfbane fructifying your virginal womb?

When he climbed into the tower and slayed your dragon, did you mourn that black beast's death? When he slid inside your womanhood as you slumbered in the stars, did you know something of love planted in the unconscious, and tell me, Sleeping Beauty, what did it feel like to make love asleep yet awake?

Floating through life from princess to captive to fool? We are flowers, we bloom, we decay, we become queens with only our thorns left to guide us long after our petals have withered.

Let your briars be your crown, my mourning dove, let he who guides you out of the tower father your babes, for otherwise, you would fall without Rapunzel's locks to guide you, and raising legends blessed by good fairies is like seeing your heart reflected in pools of moon.

Did you get everything you expected, Briar?

Is he everything you thought a prince would be?

Or is the dragon still there haunting the watchtower of your mind, licking your tears away with a burning tongue as you are paralyzed by nightmares?

To be cursed is to be whole, don't you know, my love?

I am writing this to myself to begin again, and the captive princess inside me needs to heed this advice:

Prince Charmings are deceiving, and sometimes, it is better to stay walled up, but we cannot help ourselves, for we are coated in red and prickles, and whenever we make love to ourselves, we prick our finger on spindles.

So to love yourself is to kill yourself, and to bear the flame of fairytales is to become mother to multiplicity.

Do you have the courage to come down from Migdal Eder?

Can you walk out of that enchanted forest brow proud, breasts high, pride intact?

Where does our story begin
again?

The Rules of Blind Obedience
Amirah al-Wassif

My people hate feeding
The black cats
They say these animals
Are signs of evil
They also refuse
Using salt
They believe
It is a reflection of sadness.
They also treat me
Like a great sin
They imprisoned me in a box
With an opening
For teasing me
From time to time.
I see the light
But couldn't catch it
Next to me a dead fish
Although I am starving
I can't touch it
The fish is powerless
Just like me.
The darkness presses
Against my tongue
My limbs are numb
My wings were lost in a dream.
I am waving to someone
In the mirror
Someone looks like me
In a strange way.

Who?

Jacqueline West's poetry has appeared in Mythic Delirium, Strange Horizons, Liminality, Enchanted Living, and Star*Line. Her first full-length collection, *Candle and Pins: Poems on Superstitions,* was released in 2018 (Hiraeth Publishing). She is also the author of the NYT-bestselling middle grade series The Books of Elsewhere, the YA horror novel Last Things, and several other award-winning books for young readers. A three-time nominee for both the Rhysling Award and the Pushcart Prize, Jacqueline lives with her family in Red Wing, Minnesota.

Darrell Lindsey is the author of three poetry collections, the most recent being Spectrum (Cyberwit.net, 2020).

His work has appeared in more than 75 journals, magazines, and anthologies. He lives in Nacogdoches, the oldest town in Texas.

Amirah al-Wassif says I am an award-winning published poet living in Egypt. My poetry collection "For Those Who Don't Know Chocolate" was published in February 2019 by Poetic Justice Books & arts. My illustrated children book: The Cocoa Boy and Other Stories was published in February 2020. My poem "Hallucinations" was nominated for the Science Fiction Poetry Rhysling Award

My poems have appeared in several prints and online publications including South Florida Poetry, Birmingham Arts Journal, Hawaii Review, The Meniscus, Chiron Review, The Hunger, Writers Resist, Right Now, and several other publications.

Zoe Davis is an emerging writer and avid doodler from Sheffield, England. A Quality Engineer in advanced manufacturing by day, she spends her evenings and weekends writing poetry and prose, and especially enjoys exploring the interaction between the fantastical and the mundane, with a deeply personal edge to her work. You can find her words in publications such as: Acropolis Journal, MONO. Hungry Shadow Press and Hearth & Coffin. When she's not writing, Zoe enjoys baking, crochet and playing para ice hockey- just not at the same time. You can follow her on X @MeanerHarker where she's always happy to have a virtual coffee and a chat.

Stephanie Smith is a poet and writer from Scranton, Pennsylvania. Her work has appeared in such publications as Abyss & Apex, The Horror Zine, Raven Cage, The Chamber, Aphelion, And Liquid Imagination.

www.ingramcontent.com/pod-product-compliance
Lightning Source LLC
LaVergne TN
LVHW021953060526
838201LV00049B/1693